MAIN

D0959140

SAMANTHA'S SPECIAL TALENT

SAMANTHA · 1904

BY SARAH MASTERS BUCKEY

ILLUSTRATIONS DAN ANDREASEN,
TROY HOWELL

VIGNETTES SUSAN MCALILEY

THE AMERICAN GIRLS COLLECTION®

Published by Pleasant Company Publications
Previously published in *American Girl*® magazine
Copyright © 2003 by Pleasant Company
For information, address: Book Editor, Pleasant Company Publications,
8400 Fairway Place, P.O. Box 620998, Middleton, WI 53562.

Visit our Web site at **americangirl.com**

Printed in Singapore.
03 04 05 06 07 08 09 10 TWP 10 9 8 7 6 5 4 3

The American Girls Collection® and logo, American Girls Short Stories™,
and the American Girl logo are trademarks of Pleasant Company.

Library of Congress Cataloging-in-Publication Data

Buckey, Sarah Masters, 1955–
Samantha's special talent / by Sarah Masters Buckey ; illustrations,
Dan Andreasen, Troy Howell ; vignettes, Susan McAliley.
p. cm. — (The American girls collection)
Summary: Samantha organizes a talent show to support the library, but wonders
what her special talent is. Includes historical notes on vaudeville as well as
instructions for juggling scarves.

ISBN 1-58485-693-9
[1. Talent shows—Fiction. 2. Libraries—Fiction.]
I. Andreasen, Dan, ill. II. Howell, Troy, ill. III. McAliley, Susan, ill.
IV. Title. V. Series.
PZ7.B87983 Sam 2003   [Fic]—dc21   2002029670

CHILDRENS ROOM

The
AMERICAN GIRLS
COLLECTION®

TABLE OF CONTENTS

SAMANTHA'S FAMILY
AND FRIENDS

SAMANTHA'S FAMILY

GRANDMARY
Samantha's grandmother,
who wants her to be
a young lady.

UNCLE GARD
Samantha's favorite uncle,
who calls her Sam.

AUNT CORNELIA
An old-fashioned beauty who
has newfangled ideas.

SAMANTHA
A nine-year-old orphan
who lives with her wealthy
grandmother.

IDA
*Samantha's school friend, who
is the best artist in the class.*

EDDIE
*Samantha's neighbor,
who loves to tease.*

MARGUERITE
*A shy but talented girl who
just arrived from France.*

SAMANTHA'S SPECIAL TALENT

R ain pounded the roof of the old Mount Bedford Public Library as Samantha and her friend Ida read together at a small corner table. Samantha was caught up in the adventures of an Amazon River explorer. The fearless explorer was just about to be attacked by crocodiles when—*plop!*—a drop of water landed on Samantha's head.

Samantha looked up. *Plop!* Another drop hit her eye. Water was dripping through the ceiling of the old library.

Samantha slid her book to Ida's side of the table and hurried over to the librarian, a tall, red-bearded man who was sitting at the circulation desk. Above his desk, a poster announced:

BUILD A BETTER LIBRARY!
MEETING AT 4 P.M. SATURDAY, MAY 5TH
THE MOUNT BEDFORD OPERA HOUSE

"It's leaking over there, Mr. Hardy," said Samantha, pointing to the ceiling. "I hope the library can be fixed soon."

The librarian nodded. "We're trying to raise the money, Samantha. But not many people come to our meetings. Sometimes I wonder how we'll ever get support." He sighed.

"I wish I could help," Samantha offered.

Mr. Hardy reached under his desk. He pulled out a battered tin bucket. "How about putting a bucket under that leak?"

As Samantha carried the bucket to her table, she wondered, *Why won't people come to the library meetings? Everybody always comes to our school meetings.* Suddenly an idea hit her. She hurried back to the librarian. "Mr. Hardy," she burst out, "maybe we could have a talent show!"

Mr. Hardy looked up. "Pardon?"

"We have a talent show at school every year, and all the families come," Samantha explained excitedly. "Maybe if we had a talent show at the Opera House, people would come to the library meeting."

"It's an interesting idea," Mr. Hardy said slowly. "But Saturday is only four days away. Could a talent show be organized so quickly?"

"I'm sure it could," Samantha said. "I bet lots of children would like to perform. I know *I'd* like to be in a show."

Mr. Hardy stroked his red beard. Finally he said, "I'm giving a talk to the Ladies' Club this afternoon. They might assist with a show like that. After all, any money you raise would be a help, even if—" *Plop! Plop!*

A second leak had opened in the ceiling above Mr. Hardy's desk. He grabbed another bucket to catch the rain. *Spang* went the water as it hit the tin. Mr. Hardy laughed. "Even if it's only a drop in the bucket!"

Samantha rushed to her table. "Ida, listen!" she exclaimed, and she told her friend about the proposed talent show.

Ida put down her mystery. "Jeepers, Samantha, it's a wonderful idea! I'll help make tickets."

"I thought maybe you and I could perform together," Samantha suggested. "We could dance or sing a duet or—"

"No! I could never go onstage!" Ida interrupted, shaking her head so hard, her hair swung across her face. "Besides, aren't you going to play the piano, like you always do?"

"I don't want to play the piano again," Samantha said, looking down at the scarred wooden table. "Edith Eddleton

5

always plays the piano, and she's ten times better than I am." Samantha paused. "But if we did something together . . ."

"I'm sorry, Samantha, but I'd die of fright if I had to go onstage," Ida said firmly. Suddenly thunder exploded outside. Both girls jumped. "It would be even scarier than *that*," Ida added.

The two girls giggled. Then Samantha said, "Ida, you're the best artist in the class. Would you draw posters for the show?"

"That would be easy!" Ida said. "I hope the Ladies' Club says yes to the idea."

"I hope so, too," Samantha agreed. *And,* she thought, *I hope I can think of an act to do!*

🦢

At school the next day, excitement spread when the teacher, Miss Stevens, announced there would be a children's talent show at the Opera House on Saturday afternoon.

"Samantha is helping to organize this event," Miss Stevens said. "If you would like to perform, talk to her during recess." The whole class turned to look at Samantha, who tried to smile confidently.

"The show will aid the library, so I hope you'll participate," Miss Stevens added.

Clarisse Van Sicklen, the class know-it-all, raised her hand. "How can one talent show pay for a library?" she asked skeptically.

Miss Stevens peered over her glasses. "Big projects may have small beginnings, Clarisse."

Another girl raised her hand. Samantha was surprised to see that it was Marguerite DuBois, the new student from France. Marguerite's widowed mother, Madame DuBois, taught French at Lessing's Boys School. Marguerite rarely spoke in class. When she did talk, some girls snickered at her accent.

"Mees Stevens, what ees a 'talent show'?" the French girl asked shyly.

"It's a show where girls and boys perform their special talents, such as singing or dancing," Miss Stevens explained.

"Doesn't Marguerite know anything?" Clarisse whispered, loud enough for the other girls to hear. Marguerite blushed bright red.

Miss Stevens had turned to the black-board. "Let's return to mathematics, girls. You may discuss the talent show at recess."

When the recess bell clanged, Helen Whitney hurried to Samantha's desk. "My two sisters and I sing together," she announced.

"Wonderful!" Samantha said. She pulled out a crisp sheet of new paper. "The Whitney Sisters—singing," she wrote carefully. She had her first act for the talent show!

Clarisse and Edith Eddleton marched over together. "I'll play my best piano sonata," Edith announced. "I should be first on the program since I always win the school talent show."

Samantha rolled her eyes. Edith always insisted she should be first. "I'll do my best," Samantha promised.

"Put me down for the violin," Clarisse proclaimed.

More girls clustered around Samantha's desk. Ruth Adams and Elisabeth Turner offered to perform a clarinet duo. Emmeline Andrews revealed that she could do a dramatic reading of "The Song of Hiawatha." Everyone was talking excitedly when Samantha noticed Marguerite sitting alone at her desk.

"Marguerite, would you like to be in the show?" Samantha asked.

"Her?" Clarisse sneered. "She doesn't even know what a talent show is!"

The French girl blushed again. Samantha's own face grew hot. "Don't pay attention, Marguerite," Samantha said. "Clarisse just wishes she could speak French as well as you do."

Clarisse tossed her head. "Come on, let's go outside," she urged Edith and the others. They filed out, leaving Samantha and Marguerite alone in the classroom.

Samantha walked over to Marguerite. "Would you like to dance in the show? Miss Stevens said you took ballet lessons in Paris."

"To go onstage alone—it is difficult, yes?" Marguerite asked.

"Yes—I mean no!" Samantha exclaimed. "It's fun, and it's for a good cause."

"I would need music," Marguerite said. "At home, my mother plays the violin when I dance. Yet she gives lessons on Saturdays. I do not know if she could play at a show."

"If your mother can't come, I'll play the piano for you," Samantha volunteered.

Marguerite's face brightened. "*Merci,*

Samantha! Are you sure?"

"I'm sure." Samantha added to her list "Marguerite—ballet."

After school, several neighborhood boys signed up for the show. Ida's brother, Winston, said that he would do his "famous magic act." Fred Whitney insisted that his talking parrot, Pete, should perform. Henry Van Sicklen bragged that he played trumpet "better than any kid in Mount Bedford." Even Samantha's bratty neighbor, Eddie Ryland, wanted to be included in the show.

"I can juggle better than anyone," Eddie declared. "I'm bound to win first prize."

By the end of the day, Samantha had ten acts scheduled. As she and Grandmary sat in the parlor that evening, she proudly displayed her list of performers.

"You've worked very hard," Grandmary said. "But I don't see your name on this list."

"If Madame DuBois can't come to the show, I'll play for Marguerite," Samantha replied. She looked down. "I can't think of any act to do on my own. I don't have any special talents."

"You're a very talented young lady," Grandmary said gently. "Have faith in your abilities."

Samantha thought about what Grandmary had said. Before bedtime, she wrote a list of her talents to see if one might be useful in the show:

My Talents

Singing — I'm good, but Helen
and her sisters are better!

Piano — I'm quite good, but
Edith is much better.

Boating — I'm good, but there's
no lake at the Opera House!

Reading — I'm very good, but
I don't like reading aloud.

What should I do? Samantha wondered.
I have to think of something by Saturday!

But during the next two days, Samantha
was so busy organizing the show, she had
no time to plan an act. After school Thurs-
day, she and Ida made posters and put them
up around town. Samantha noticed that her
posters looked plain compared with Ida's,
which had fancy lettering and borders.

15

"How do you make yours so pretty?"

"I've always liked drawing," Ida said with a shrug. "It's just a talent, I suppose."

I wish I knew what my talent was, Samantha thought.

After school Friday, Samantha and Ida invited Marguerite to help make tickets. *"Oui!"* she agreed, her eyes glistening with happiness.

The three girls sat under a tree in Ida's yard with ginger cookies and glasses of milk. While they folded and cut, Samantha asked Marguerite if her mother could play in the show.

"She will come if she must," said Marguerite as she maneuvered her scissors through the paper.

"I've always liked drawing," Ida said with a shrug.
"It's just a talent, I suppose."

17

"She has lessons to teach, though, so it would be difficult. Perhaps we should practice with the piano at the rehearsal tonight. Do you know *Swan Lake*?"

"No, but it won't be a problem," Samantha said confidently. *I'm not as good as Edith, but I can play the piano,* she thought.

The three girls worked and chatted until Samantha looked up and saw the sun glowing red on the horizon. "Oh, no!" she said. "We'll be late to rehearsal!"

Ida stayed behind to arrange the tickets while Samantha and Marguerite brushed grass off their dresses and hurried to the Opera House. The Ladies' Club had asked Miss Stevens, who produced the school shows, to direct the rehearsal. The teacher was watching each act with a critical eye.

"Louder, girls!" she told the Whitney sisters. "Sing so everyone will hear you!"

Miss Stevens advised Fred to put a leash on his parrot. "Your parrot may become nervous when it performs," she cautioned.

Glancing around the big Opera House, Samantha realized she might become nervous, too. Marguerite's dance was the last act of the show, and as the girls waited to rehearse, Samantha studied the music. It looked harder than she had expected. *I wish I'd had time to practice,* she thought.

When Miss Stevens finally called them up, Marguerite jumped gracefully onto the wooden stage. Samantha wiped her sweating palms and sat at the big piano.

19

She quickly discovered that *Swan Lake* was even harder than it looked. As she struggled to find the notes, she kept losing the tempo. *Marguerite may be a swan,* Samantha thought, *but I feel like a turtle.*

"Faster, Samantha," Miss Stevens urged.

Samantha tried, but it was no use. The more she and Marguerite worked to keep pace with each other, the more they both seemed out of step.

Most of the other performers had gone home, but Eddie Ryland had stayed to practice juggling. Now he sneered at the girls. "You call that dancing? My dog dances better!"

"Go home, Eddie," said Miss Stevens.

As soon as Eddie left, Samantha

Eddie sneered at the girls.
"You call that dancing? My dog dances better!"

stopped playing. "We need your mother," she told Marguerite glumly. The other girl nodded.

"It ees not easy, Samantha," Marguerite said comfortingly. "Thank you for trying."

Samantha felt like crying. *I'm not good at anything,* she thought. But she tried to act cheerful. "It's probably just as well I won't be playing the piano tomorrow," she said. "Ida and I will be busy selling tickets."

Saturday turned out to be even more hectic than Samantha had imagined. So many friends and family members lined up for the show that Samantha and Ida sold more than a hundred tickets.

"Jiminy!" Samantha exclaimed when she saw all the money they had collected. "That should help the library fund. Let's go see the show!"

Grandmary had saved the girls two front-row seats. They slid into them just in time for Edith's piano sonata. Samantha felt a stab of jealousy as she listened to Edith's nearly perfect performance. *Everyone is more talented than I am,* she thought.

Not all the acts went perfectly, however. Emmeline forgot a verse of "Hiawatha," Clarisse's violin squeaked, and the Whitney sisters sang so softly, they could barely be heard. Fred's big green parrot tried to fly away, but luckily Fred had put him on a leash.

23

Winston's magic show went smoothly until he reached dramatically into his black hat to pull out a rabbit. The rabbit, however, popped out from under the table and scampered across the stage. The audience clapped and laughed.

The next act was Eddie Ryland's juggling. Samantha was impressed by his skill. He managed three balls and made it look easy.

The last act was Marguerite's ballet solo. Marguerite entered the stage wearing a full white skirt that looked like a real ballerina's, but she seemed pale and nervous.

Samantha crossed her fingers. *I encouraged her to do this,* she thought. *I hope it goes well.*

As Madame DuBois played the opening notes, Marguerite took a deep breath and began to dance. At first she seemed unsure of herself. But as the music continued, she moved with greater confidence. Finally, like a bird that has just learned to fly, Marguerite soared across the stage, her shimmering skirt swirling with every turn and leap.

When she took her bow, the audience applauded enthusiastically. Samantha and Ida exchanged happy smiles.

As the judges put their heads together, Samantha squirmed in her seat. She wanted so much for Marguerite to do well! Finally, the judges gave their results to Mr. Hardy.

The librarian cleared his throat. "As I announce the winners, please come onstage. Third prize . . . Edward Ryland." Eddie swaggered up to receive a handsome bronze medal. Samantha sighed. It was a shame anyone as mean as Eddie should win anything.

Mr. Hardy continued, "Second prize . . . Marguerite DuBois." Samantha clapped so hard, she almost fell off her seat. *I bet Clarisse won't make fun of Marguerite now!* she thought.

Marguerite shyly accepted a beautiful silver medal, while Madame DuBois beamed.

Mr. Hardy held up a fancy gold medal. "For first prize . . . Edith Eddleton!"

Samantha applauded. Edith was annoying, but she did play the piano beautifully.

After the applause faded, Mr. Hardy held up his hand. "Before we talk about the library, I'd like Samantha Parkington to come up."

Samantha looked about in surprise. *He can't mean me,* she thought. *I wasn't even in the show.* Grandmary, however, nudged her gently. Reluctantly, she climbed onto the stage.

"Today's talent show was Samantha's idea, and she helped organize it," Mr. Hardy announced. "I'm grateful for the money raised, and I'm impressed by Samantha's talents as a leader."

Samantha felt her face flush. Looking

*"Today's talent show was Samantha's idea,
and she helped organize it," Mr. Hardy announced.*

at the audience, she saw Grandmary
watching her with fond, proud eyes.
*I guess Grandmary was right—I do have a
special talent*, she thought. The audience
clapped loudly.

Mr. Hardy smiled. "I'm all out of
medals, Samantha. But if you come to the
library on Monday, you can be the first
person to get a card for the new library
we're going to build."

"That would be wonderful," Samantha
said with a grin. "Reading is one of my
best talents!"

29

SARAH MASTERS BUCKEY

At 9   Now

When I was 14, I got my first job, working as a "page," or aide, at our local library. I loved books, so I enjoyed everything about the job—except having to be quiet. I also loved to talk!

Sarah Masters Buckey is also the author of the History Mysteries titles **Enemy in the Fort** *and* **The Smuggler's Treasure***.*

Looking
Back
1904

A PEEK INTO THE PAST

*Great
Acts in
1904*

In the early 1900s, before the invention of television or movies with sound, the most popular form of entertainment was *vaudeville* [VAWD-vil], a kind of "variety" show.

Like Samantha's talent show, a vaudeville show had many different acts. Performers sang, danced, told jokes, did magic and acrobatic tricks, and showed off trained animals.

Ventriloquists carried on conversations with wooden dummies.

Vaudeville was entertainment for everyone. Theater managers banned words like "slob" and "son of a gun" from the acts so that women and children could attend. Tickets were inexpensive, so middle- and even lower-class people could afford them. And vaudeville houses welcomed people of all nationalities onstage and in the audience.

There were many sister acts in vaudeville.

Some African Americans found success in vaudeville, like comedian Bert Williams. He performed in *blackface*, makeup once worn by white performers to imitate black people. Black performers were required to wear blackface, too, because that was what white audiences expected to see. With his shabby suit and hat and oversized shoes, Williams poked fun not at his own race but at situations that everyone could relate to. He quickly became a star, and he paved the way for other black performers as well.

Vaudeville was a place where women

Offstage, Bert Williams was poised and polished.

were paid as much as, if not more than, men, especially stars like Lillian Russell and Eva Tanguay. Singer

Lillian Russell wore expensive, elegant costumes and won over audiences with her voice, beauty, and grace. Eva Tanguay, in contrast, wore outrageous costumes and pranced across the stage as she belted out her songs. She sang and danced so energetically that she was compared to a tornado!

Eva Tanguay

COMING

MYSTIC MACK CO.

LATEST MAGIC

Marvelous Balancing Acts

See the Great Sack and Shackle Escape Act

Floating Ball and Spirit Hand

Music and Singing by a Lady Radio Artist

EVERYTHING NEW

Don't Miss This Show

TO-NIGHT

Vaudeville audiences were also fascinated with magic acts. Magicians at the turn of the century read people's minds, made animals appear and disappear, suspended bodies in the air, and sawed people in half only to "rejoin" them at the end of the act. But the greatest vaudeville magician was really an escape artist—Harry Houdini.

Card tricks were one of the most popular magic acts.

Houdini could escape from any pair of handcuffs, often in a few minutes or even seconds. He escaped from locked trunks and straitjackets, too. Eventually, he made his escape act more daring by doing it underwater. With his hands chained, Houdini crouched inside a milk can that was filled

Houdini amazed police officers with his "magical" escapes.

with water and locked shut. Several minutes later, a wet and breathless Houdini would emerge from the can— much to the relief of the audience!

Vaudeville greats like Bert Williams, Eva Tanguay, and Harry Houdini inspired many children to enter vaudeville. Some vaudeville houses offered amateur nights, where young performers could test their talents onstage. On a good night, an amateur act might get the most applause and win a cash prize. On a bad night, an act might disappoint the audience and get "the hook"—a long crooked pole that was used to pull performers right off the stage!

Anna and Lillian Roth had an amateur sister act.

Hooks were long enough to reach performers from either side of the stage.

Comedian Fanny Brice began her vaudeville career in an amateur contest in 1906. When the contestant before her got the hook, someone pushed 14-year-old Fanny onstage. Fanny's act won the contest's five-dollar prize, and she scooped up another five dollars in coins that the appreciative audience had thrown onstage. Fanny started performing in vaudeville houses all over New York City and eventually became one of the most famous female comedians.

"Funny woman" Fanny Brice

Other young stars were born into vaudeville—their parents were performers. These children learned at an early age how to juggle, dance, tell jokes, and sing. Little Buster Keaton joined his mother and father's act almost as soon as he could walk. Carried onstage in a suitcase, the little boy charmed audiences. As a young man, Buster brought his comedy to movies in Hollywood.

The Three Keatons— Buster and his parents

The Palace Theatre was the most famous vaudeville house in America.

Movies eventually brought about the end of vaudeville. The Palace Theatre in New York, where Samantha might have seen vaudeville as a young woman, began showing movies in the early 1930s. Other vaudeville houses followed suit. Sadly, the death of vaudeville meant the end of some of the greatest acts—dancers, singers, and comedians—of all time.

LEARN TO JUGGLE
Scarves make juggling easy and fun!

Juggling was a popular trick in vaudeville, especially for children. Jugglers used everything from balls to wooden bicycle rims, or "hoops," when they performed. Some performers combined juggling with clowning to make their acts more fun for audiences.

Try juggling using chiffon scarves. Once you've mastered the trick, you'll be ready for your next talent show!

1. Hold one scarf in your dominant hand—the hand you write with.

2. Toss the scarf by scooping your hand from the outside to the inside and letting go of the scarf when your hand is at chest height. Catch the scarf in your other hand.

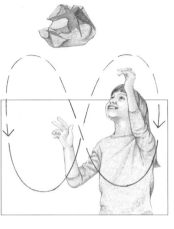

3. Toss the scarf back to your dominant hand. Practice tossing the scarf from hand to hand in a figure-eight pattern.

4. Add a second scarf, holding it in your non-dominant hand.

5. Toss the first scarf in the air, and just as it begins to come down, toss the second scarf.

6. Practice tossing the scarves back and forth until you can do it smoothly and are comfortable starting with either hand.

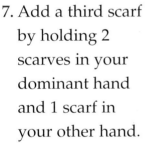

7. Add a third scarf by holding 2 scarves in your dominant hand and 1 scarf in your other hand.

8. Toss one of the scarves in your dominant hand into the air. When that scarf begins to come down, toss the scarf from your other hand into the air.

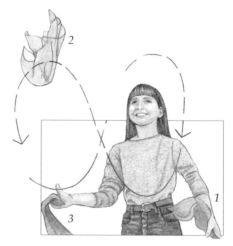

9. As you catch the first scarf, toss the third scarf into the air. Always keep one scarf in the air. Keep tossing and catching until you have a steady rhythm.

American Girl®

PO BOX 620497
MIDDLETON WI 53562-0497

American Girl ®

Catalogue Request

Join our mailing list! Just drop this card
in the mail, call **1-800-845-0005**, or visit
our Web site at **americangirl.com**.

Send me a catalogue:

Name

Address

City   State   Zip 1961i

Girl's birth date:

_____ / _____ / _____
month day year

Send my friend a catalogue.

Name

Address

City   State   Zip 1225i

E-mail

Parent's signature